GEMS OF KINTSUGI

BHAVYA BHATEJA

Made with ♥ on the Notion Press Platform
www.notionpress.com

My Family has been an integral part of me . They have supported me whenever I needed it . This is to the ones who have always had

my back !

Contents

Contents

Preface

Kintsugi , also known as kintsukuroi is the Japanese art of repairing broken objects by mending the areas of breakage with lacquer gold, silver, or platinum; the method is similar to the maki-e technique. As a philosophy, it treats breakage and repair as part of the history of an object, rather than something to disguise.

This book is all about the broken pieces and converting them into something more valueable than Gold or any other metal . I hope you enjoy it and gather the same feelings as me .

Thank You all for showing intrest in my book !!

1. The Firsts

These are the one of the my first written poems that I'd like to share with you all . All these poems are written sitting in the school library . The level of books will keep increasing as the book progresses on .

Vision

I was now thinking for a while,

about what has been on my mind.

The many ups and downs I have been through,

Overthinking in the summer loo

I was in a trance for a while

Thinking of what was just mine

Just then , someone shook me up,

The loo went past me

I walked through the shredded trees ;

With the aim on my mind,

And vision behind .

I knew what was to be done ,

I had responsibilities of a son ....

Your Smile

I've been in a jolly mood

Can't control my feelings

I feel ; I am in Love

The smile you possess

No way , I ain't getting Impressed

I wish you were close to me

Spend moments where it's just you and me

I will be the luckiest , if you are beside me

This beautiful smile has always had me !!!

What is Love ?

What is Love , I gotta explain

Just pure feelings mixed with some pain

Love tho is not easy , peasy and chessy as it looks like

It has many waves and tides ; for sure it's not glide

You smile , You Laugh

You cry , You fly high

Love has another aspect

You gotta have mutual respect

Try and give in your best

Love God will handle the rest

Love Gods will guide you themselves

Keep your faith , Gods don't do anything less than the best

Make sure you keep the Love in the purest form

Ultimately that's the only norm ...

2. About Damn World !

This part shows how this world works . Not every ending is a ***Happy Ending*** *and not every Fairytale is* ***Cinderella*** *. We have to fight with our own* ***Demons*** *and take over this world .*

Destiny

I compared my Destiny with a few other folks

I thought mine was a complete joke

The struggles I run through every moment

I conceive it's more difficult than a Saint

Every so often I feel I need to work hard

But then I perceive that the world works smart !

The People see me smile

They don't get I am far from a million mile

I curse my own destiny,

Getting convinced mine was a complete scare

For other people I don't really care !!

Now grasping onto the real scene

I feel it was a little mean .

I apologise all you folks

For when I think my life was a joke

This life has been great to me ,

For this I thank you God :)!!

My Devil

Alo , I have a story to tell

About 'My Devil' in its nutshell

Let me take you to 'his' world

It's his life which is messed and curled

'My Archangel ' had the people's curse

'My Archangel' fell in people's verse

'My Archangel ' was overpowered by Miscreants

'My Archangel ' was let down this recent

'My Archangel' grind hard

So 'That Archangel' he could discard

And be 'The Devil' he desired

All alone in his empire

The broken man , dreaded, shredded curses the almighty

For how his life is eventually gritty

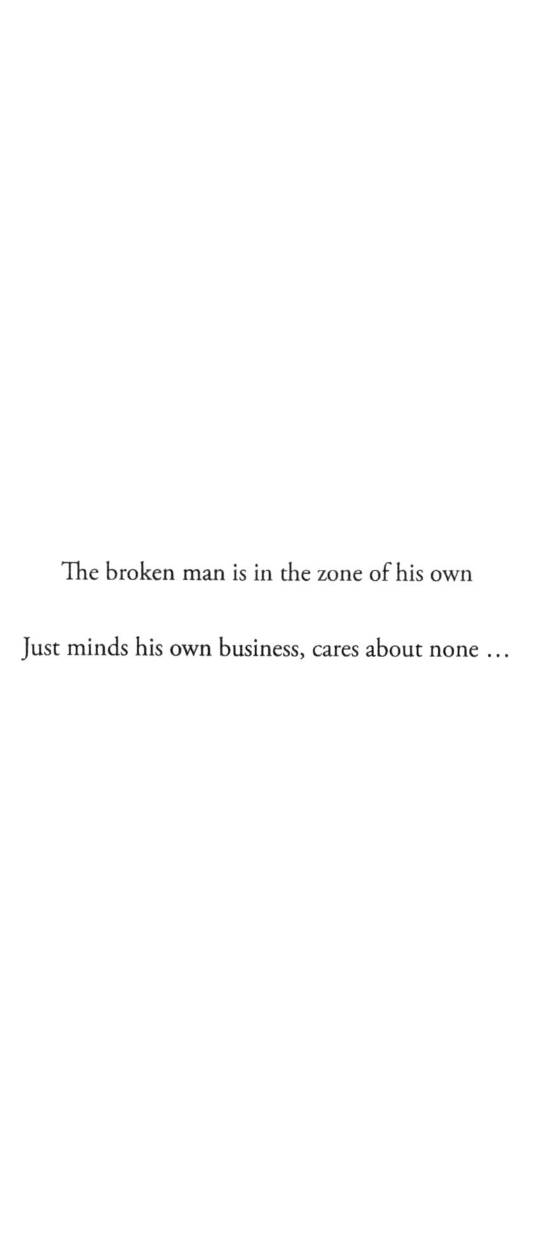

The broken man is in the zone of his own

Just minds his own business, cares about none …

The Forgotten One

Aforetime , was a forgotten warrior back in the city of warriors

Sitting on a Manja with Hookah and whiskey is how he is portrayed by historians

The people admired and applauded him for his deeds

He was a perfect man that one needs

The warrior had been successful in the recent past

He was way better than the contrast

Like a God , people used to worship him

He ruled the throne like a true king

But as they say , Good things don't last forever

He was again at the place where he belonged, to save the city from Terror

The warrior gave it all for the city and died trying

The people were shocked and the city was crying

New owner of the throne had finally arrived

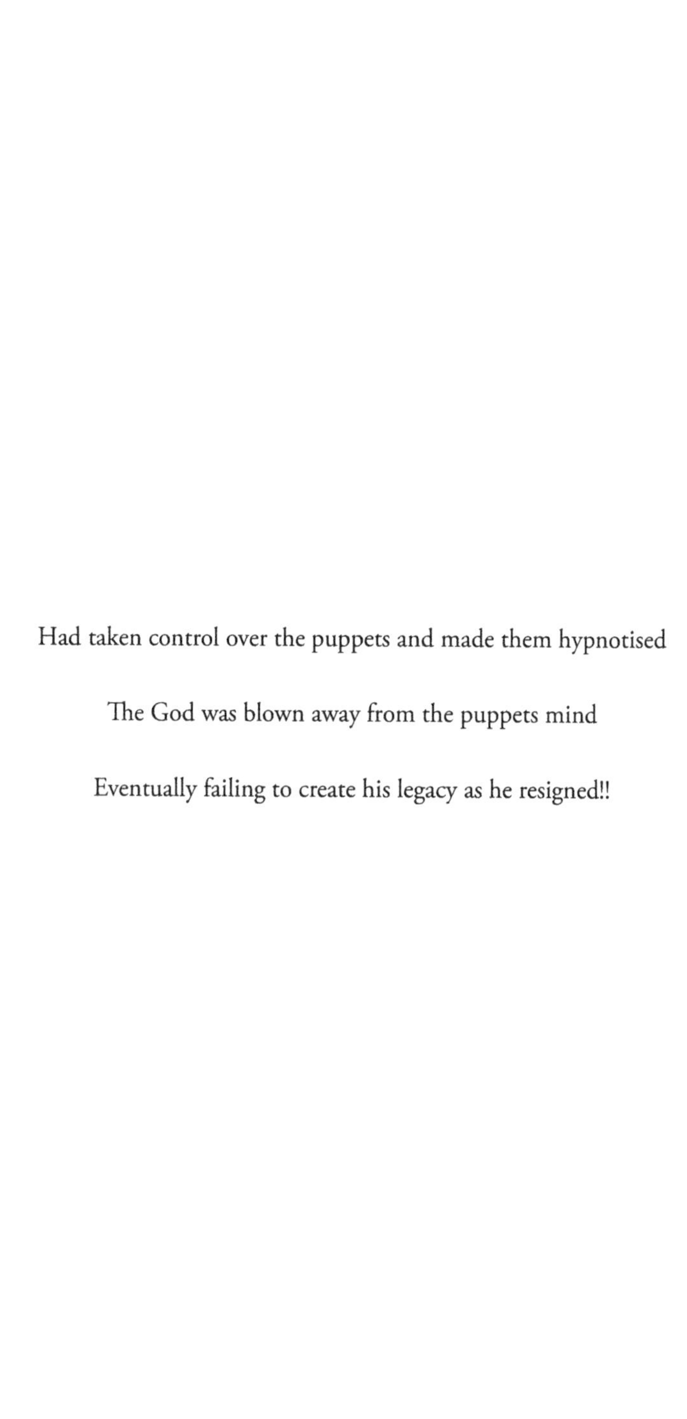

Had taken control over the puppets and made them hypnotised

The God was blown away from the puppets mind

Eventually failing to create his legacy as he resigned!!

Forbidden Truth

Hey kid , you think this world is easy to survive ?

This world is full of chaos , yet we've gotta find a way and strive

The world is a dirty competition,

Can get past any boundaries for the recognition

You talk about the love being pure

Once your heart breaks there is no cure

Here The strongest guys have been through the Deadliest Heartbreaks

Get out of that Lucid Dream and wake wake wake

They say 'Be like water my Friend'

This world is gonna mix you with anything in a mixer jar and blend

It's good to be water but better if you are an ice

Don't change your state of matter , until you find someone nice

I don't give a dam about the world that doesn't mean anything to me

Protect yourself from the world just as hives are protected by honey bee

Be very careful of who you include in your group

Or you'll end up mixing yourself in this chaotic world , and

That's the **ForbiddenTruth**

3. 3 AM Therapy

*This segment is all about the motivation you desire in your life. These are the poems you wanna read at midnight and get motivated. Presenting you the '**3 AM Thearpy**'*

The Era

New Year , but same old me

Time for 'A New Era ' to begin

Time to change the pattern of the game

Let the tables turn around

In this era I will make myself proud

There ain't any room for self doubt

Time to change process into progress

Little by little, day by day making myself more efficient

The silenced storm in me is waiting for an opportunity to burst

I'll come out like a molten lava on the earth

You'll be telling generations about 'This Era' gossiping under a tree

I'll bet you on this ' This Era ' will be ruled by me :)!!!!

The Warrior

The warrior was looking down at the hell

I Guess the things weren't going very well

The Warrior was looking for the good days to arrive

Soon he found out for that he'll have to strive

The warrior started to find the things that weren't going right

So he could work on them and toil hard day and night

The warrior created a vision to go beyond stars

The plan was, toil hard ; and break all bars

The warrior got distracted by none

Coming into the limelight, yet he was undone

The warrior went past the vision he had

For the Future generations to see, he had greatest theories to add !!

About the Cosmos

Gritty, Determined is what I would like to call myself

Not giving a fu*k to the world like a deaf

Confidence levelling up day by day

People taunting me , who the sh*t are they ?

Confidence converting into overconfidence takes no time

Ultimately it costed me the worst crime

Down , down and beneath the earth

My confidence shaking like a pendulum back and forth

Ups and downs are a part and parcel of the game

I was all in to get my fame

I potentially will improve with time

Get better like an old wine

I promise to justify the talent I have

God , please give me another chance I wanna make a comeback with a bang !!!

The Silent Tree and The Echoing Wind

'The Silent Tree' wasn't silent as usual

He was a lot different ecstatic like he met someone very beautiful

It was the Echoing Wind that had done wonders on the tree

Which was sweet as sugar and beneficial as green tea

The veterans say the tree used to be jolly a lil time ago

He used to be the finest and had the best glow

But once the tree got cursed by a broken man

Who used to smile from outside and cry a lot from inside

The curse of 'that broken man' was finally broken

Who used to sit under the tree saddened and heartbroken

The echoing wind has started heal the tree with her soothing voice

The tree again has started to enjoy and rejoice

Each time the echoing wind passes through The silent tree

The tree then surely gets some inspiration to be back again and be lordly

Midnight

Scattered, Shattered ; felt like I was on a roller coaster ride

The ride that only went downhill like a one way tide

The fire inside me again started to burn

Felt like my setbacks put the fuel to the dying fire to burn

They surely conceived I have the tendency to learn

Aah ! It's finally midnight thinking about this

Anticipating my journey is a pure bliss

My eyes closed and me visualising my empire and me on my throne

Out of all others I have outshone

It's now the time to perform and get my visualised throne

It's now the time to get past those unknown

When I will finally have the throne ,

I wanna look back and see how much I have grown

I wanna be proud of myself and say

'Although, Mornings show how we are enjoying our beautiful ride

But nights do all the hard work and turn the tide '

Bars for the Future

Upon reflection, this will be the best generation I've ever known

Standing for themselves, getting things done on their own

There was no one else capable of doing the things they did

Thinking out of the Box, Creative Minds; everything they did was splendid

Taking the world on a journey of success

Little by little moving forward and making progress

Future generations have a legacy to carry on

The responsibility is theirs to carry out

The time will come when they'll stand on the big stage

It should only they and their passion that they ever engage

It was this generation's way of doing things

The Bars are set up for the future Queens and Kings !!

4. An Ode to my Friends

My friends have been the stronges part of me. We've been through many ups and downs together and will be facing many challenges ahead in the future. Even though I'll be short of words, but have tried my best to dedicate them with a few lines

Dear Best Friend

Dear Bestie , you are such a cute soul

Filled with a lot of emotions inside

You are here in my life to play an important role

You are like a map to my world, or maybe a guide

Why don't you see yourself as the best ?

I'm down under the hell when I see you stressed

Why are you always sad thinking about the things not in your plan

Take a break, things will be better in a short span

Why cry when you have a heart catching smile to admire

Why cry when you have the world at large to inspire..

Time spent with you is the most precious

If I tell you something please don't feel embarrass

I love teasing you and making you jealous

But on a serious note, Thank You for always being on my side

And always for bearing my silly side

Misfits

Mysteriously I feel sad and great being alonc

Trust me you being you will be by far best known

No peer pressure, all in your zone

I declare my best friend my phone

My life seems more dark than the dark mode in phone

All the curiosity seems to have flown

No best friends, nothing at all

My life seems to have taken a fall

I desire to stand tall

Friends by my side , dancing together at a city hall

Not just at good times ; but when we breach the protocols

Standing together we can get past the Ozone

Nightmares

I used to have nightmares seeing something like demons

Often troubling me for many different reasons

They used to horror me more and more as I go deep in my thoughts

I surrendered to them and accepted my loss

I was like a slave to them

Not even dared to harm em

Until these bastards came out of nowhere as my saviours

Then uplifted me and not accept my failures

I was attracted to them by their joyous smiles

Their euphonious voice is that unique that I get to know of them coming from a million mile

If this world is a river , I wanna flow with them

If this world is ending , I wanna die with them

I call them Jaan by love

‘ They are my Yaar ‘ who I’ll always love

Chaotic Friends

My friends are the most chaotic characters in a certain way

All are jokers as the people around me say

They'll make , you cry and make you laugh

In other words I'll say ' they are my better half '

Merrily they have fun and roam all around the town

Not many people know , but there's other side as well of these clowns

They Walk the same, talk the same

Stay the same, f*ck the fame, never change

You'll have them by your side when no one else is

I can rely on them to listen to me , even when I am not in my senses

They are cute , they are sweet

When together we all can beat the heat

Emotional tears are shed for their crushes

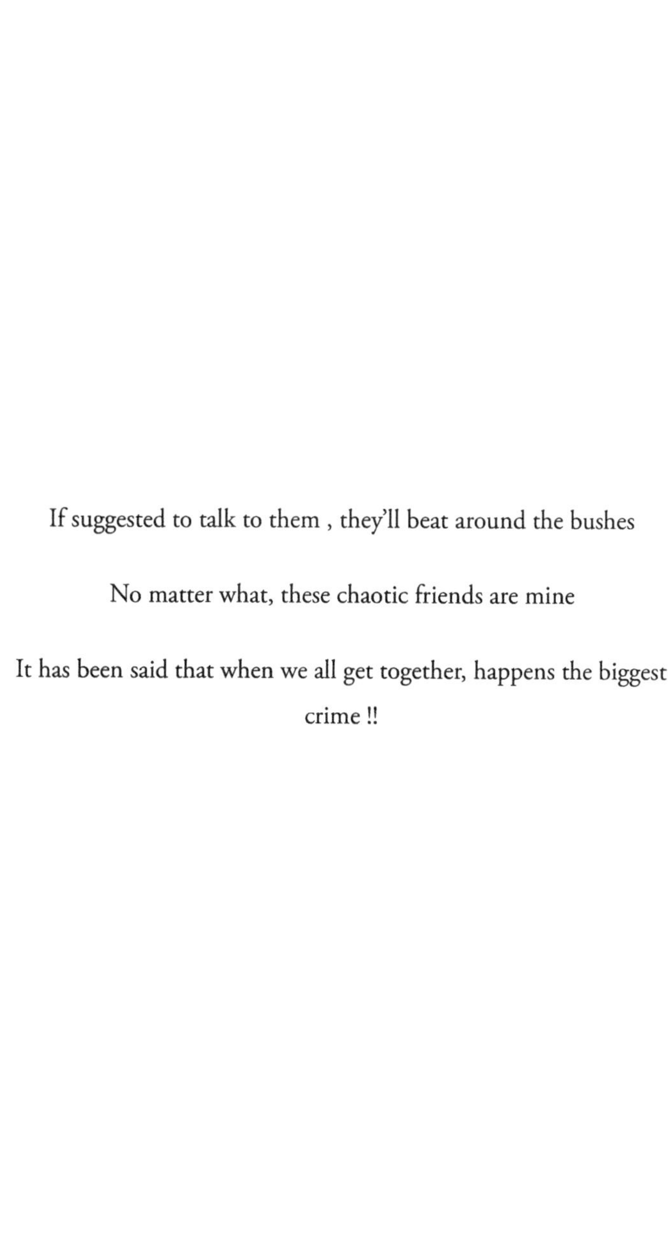

If suggested to talk to them , they'll beat around the bushes

No matter what, these chaotic friends are mine

It has been said that when we all get together, happens the biggest
crime !!

5. Love , the legacy

Love , is an important part of our lives . It encompasses a range of strong and positive emotional and mental states, from the most sublime virtue or good habit, the deepest interpersonal affection, to the simplest pleasure . This part is all about love , you'll surely feel attached and hopefully relate .

Despration

I am the moon , and maybe also some stars

Then why am I not with someone who thinks for me in the same
in the same cause

In a world where relationships are full of lies

Why am I so desperate to find a soul like a butterfly ?

Why don't I have someone with whom I could share my feelings

Why can't I admire her when she sings

I grudge my friends as they go out for a date

Why am I desperate , or am I too late ?

Little by little I cure myself

Why do I mostly miss you in the night itself

In a world where relationships are full of lies

Why am I so desperate to find a soul like a butterfly ?

To you , through him

You are my lil secret that no one knows about

Just a mutual friend between us who knows the things in and out

For me he is the saviour , he is next to God

He is my key to you , for me he is a secret code

You aren't happy with him in between

So Let me sort it out for you my queen

You my love is the best thing ever happened to me

I wish we could talk all day long sitting under a tree

But Darling, We are still too young to confess our relationship in public

Even if we do , there will be eyes on us like a Sputnik

We still in school, waiting for the holidays to arrive in June

Till then control your emotions and don't be all over the moon

Till then let my saviour save us

Or you know the consequences, so please don't rush

Till then To you , through himm !!!

Angel Baby

The last time my soul slept well

Came in my dreams a cute , bright Angel

a lil jolly and shy nature!!

Not so often I do not have that angel on my mind,

I've got a sense, for it I need to grind.

Thinking of her , I got many sleepless nights ;

To be her's , I can fly as high as kites !

I am gonna move around the world elated;

Just to find her ; and ask if she waited?

My cosy eyes show I made a sacrifice

I've got nothing but her to glorify.

Now , I can sleep fine

Knowing she is all mine

Feels like it's a fiction

Hell no , it’s a f***in addiction!!!

Stars

Stargazing the stars, lost in the sky

My mind can't get enough of you , I am lost in your eyes

A starry night , Laid Down on the top of the hill

When you are there with me , why does everything fell so still ?

A gentle breeze blowing , you lookin above in the skies

As usual you are all smiles but I am still lost in your eyes

It's a 'Never Again ' moment we've got to share

I don't want this night to ever disappear

I don't want The Dawn to ruin the night

When the sun rises , shall we go for a boat ride

We'll be back to the hill when the sun sets

Enjoying the day, having no regrets

Laying down again , again watching the skies

And me again all lost in your hypnotic eyes:)!!!

Let's talk with our Eyes

I dreamt of my darling last night

Next to the bone fire , holding each other tight

Two beautiful eyes making a contact and blushing

All silence between them and speaking nothing

Our eyes talking to each other , making thing's picturesque

Leaving her feels like a hard consequence

Her absence makes me suffer

We fell incomplete without each other

The cozy atmosphere around ,

But I wanna break silence and shout aloud

I will be by your side, each and every time

I promise you a Candle Light Dinner each time we dine

I want your head on my shoulder each time you sleep

I hope you don't mind if I steal your hoodies!!

A Magic Spell

Grinding through the years , fighting all alone

My life was an entire mess until I wanted to make you my own

Two Contrasting Characters we two are I Suppose

Me 'A cute Angry Bird' and you as special as ' The Rose '

You cast a Magic Spell as a Magician

I wanna see you before doing anything, like a superstition

Eye Catching Killer smile you possess

I surely have something to Confess

Do you mind , if I ask you to be mine

We'll spend our time all alone , with some 'Red Wine'

A Cloud

You are just like a cloud that romanticises a boring sky

I stare you like I do drugs ; I am so high

I imagine us doing a night trek to the mountain top

All lost in our convos , laughing ; finally reaching our desired stop

The Moon , The romantic clouds and The stars have been waiting
for us all this time

They all have been waiting for me to make you mine

Holding each other's hands and blushing on the mountain top will
still be the best view

I mean, Even tho it will be dark , I would still be looking at you

Your voice seems to be as soothing as a nightingale

Our love story will be more than just a fairytale

Yours

When the lights are dull and pretty dark in the room

I want to zoom in the future to be your future bridegroom

Those sparkling grey eyes attract me the most

For those interesting eyes I am ready to marry a ghost

Having you around feels like a classic Bollywood film

The wind swirling around and the traditional hymn

Your arms in mine , walking and having all the fun

Then being cozy by the bone fire with a glass of rum

Your sleepy head on my shoulder, is all what I need

If you are my addiction, then what the hell is weed :))!!

God has sent me to take care of you

Your portrait on my Back I have got it tattooed !!

My Girl

My Girl ;sarcastic sweet and not so tall

But still overhead me , you and all

Marble grey eyes take me by surprise

Her nature is as cool as an ice

A Mole on her chin ; always attracting nose pin

Feels like my wish was completed by a Jinn

I am the star that shines bright

And she being the sun that always provides me light

Seeing her cry makes me feel I have a dent

I'll always be by her side 1000 percent !!!

6. Lost Soul

Heartbreak is the one down we all face in our lives , you must have gone through many lows at that point of time . This part is all about how we feel during that period and it's not always the way we think .

Justice for you !

You say I didn't treat you well

Ohh sorry, that I made your life so hell

Justice for you ; you broke my heart for them

I see you just wanted to follow the trend !

You tell me you are all over the moon

Haha ! I will see that too soon

Crying alone saturated

Starting to feel the world getting seperated

My friends keep asking me why am I not with you

I say I cannot answer that through

Materialistic Pleasure was all that you desired

It sounds fun , but is quiet weird

I wanted to see you fly ,

High above the skies

Just can't get enough of thinking of you

Feels caged like the animals in the Zoo .

You say I didn't treat you well

Ohh sorry, that I made your life so hell !!!

Too Young to Die for You

We were a couple for the world to cherish

It was like pouring mud on a lotus , to make me more embellished

Your plans, however, were different

I knew you'd break my heart , but moving on would be difficult

The Fairytale isn't a fairytale anymore

My life either hasn't been erotic cause the way you Ignore

I thought you as my inspiration

But I regret you couldn't gather that indication

I'd have been an innocent teen , had you not left me

You are the reason behind my poetry

I Wouldn't have been able to write how badly I wanted you back
in my life

You not with me was an unusual sight for my eyes

I have no more reasons to love you

And I am still ' **Too young to die for you** '

The Last Rain Together

The Last Rain together was a whole new vibe

Us in the forests ; there's a lot I wanna write

The cloudy skies , and your marble eyes

The weather was perfect for the moment to romanticise

I just wanted you to close your eyes

I regret I couldn't plan a surprise

Under an umbrella , we stood tall looking at each other

As the day progressed , I did want to plan a supper

I fell for you more and more as we walked

I wished you stay the same as we laughed and talked !!

You were the most romantic that day

The best part was your head on my shoulder ; your arms in mine and the way we slayed

But the annoying part is that scene is hard to portray

I wish we still were together forever

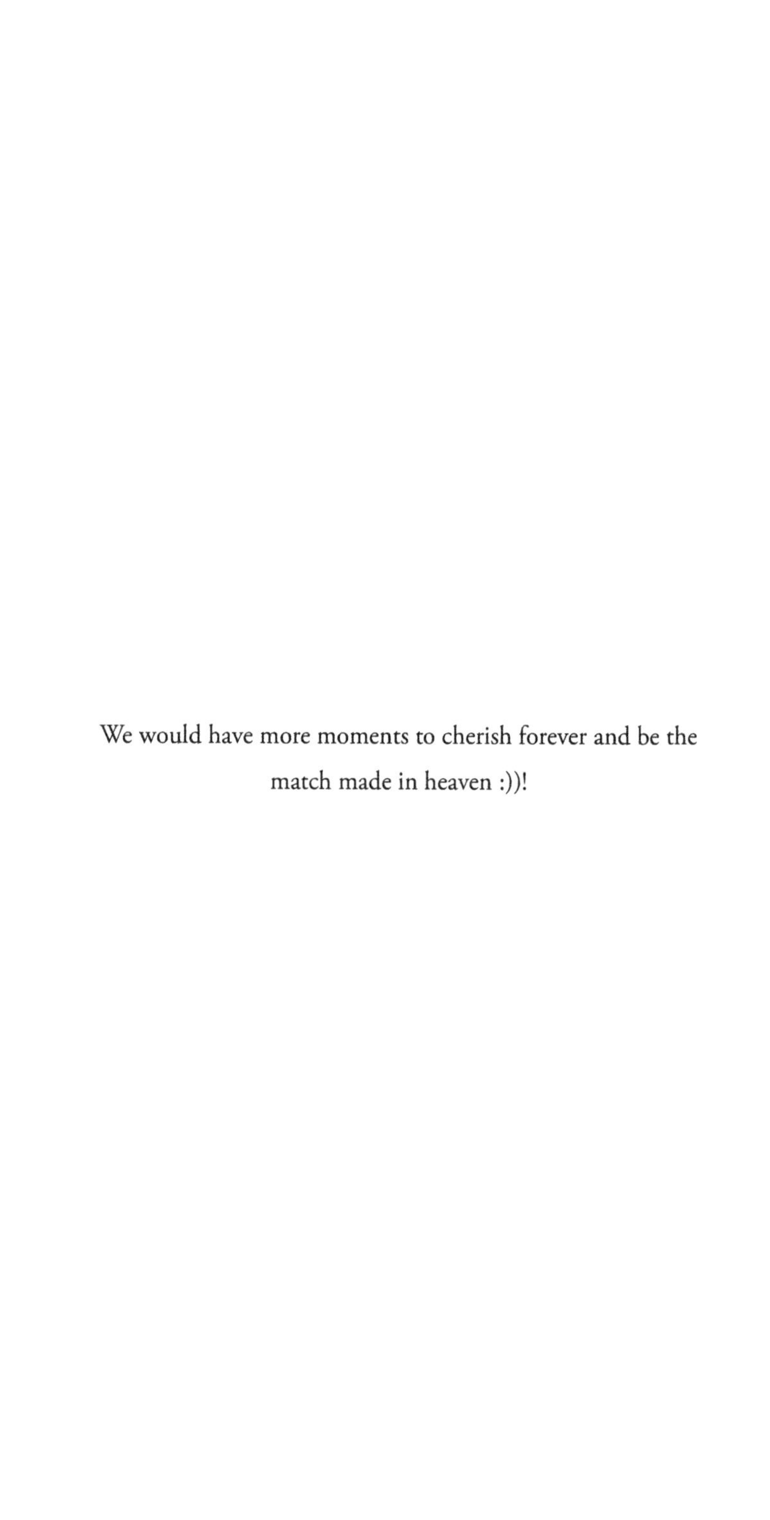

We would have more moments to cherish forever and be the match made in heaven :))!

Marrying a Ghost for You

After treasuring love for a long long time

I decided to marry a ghost , who was a lover of mine

We used to vibe together, feel better

And for a change I used to upset her

Things were well until she fell for me

Gee ! I didn't want to take things so far

Making my life so bizarre

I failed to understand her efforts

She was so alone like a tree in the desert

Now when she is gone , I understand what she went through

Valuing her more and more as the events pass through

Now I plan to marry her , if she allows

For meeting her I can go beyond the clouds !!!

Dying Midnight For You

Would you be so kind as to accept me back , out of the blue ?

Cause , I have been Dying Midnight for you

Yes , the fault was mine , to be honest I wasn't fine

I lost you for the worst is a fact I wouldn't decline

You didn't need to see my life rampageous

You deserved something way better and something advantageous

This pretty soul deserves a splendid lifestyle like a queen

Those pretty eyes didn't need tears to be seen

I went stargazing the sky without the stars in the sky

For me to leave you was the hardest Goodbye

I've been scattered since the day we parted our ways

I'll never be able to recover myself from that phase

It's been a while now since we last talked

It's very hard to rediscover myself , cause I am all lost

I had you there in my worst , will you be there in my best ?

My feelings are complex, and I have a lot to express

I still loved you then , I still love you now

I wanna be back with you anyhow

Would you be so kind as to accept me back , out of the blue ?

Cause , I have been Dying Midnight for you !!

Printed by Libri Plureos GmbH in Hamburg,
Germany